To Oonagh, my super-baby.—C.D.

For Nikki, Makiah, Elijah, and our dog, Kirby.—A.R.

Book design by Stuart Smith

Printed in the United States of America

First Edition

1 3 5 7 9 10 8 6 4 2

Library of Congress Cataloging-in-Publication Data on file.

ISBN 978-1-4231-1555-7

Visit www.disneybooks.com

Disney
BOLT

One Ridonculous Adventure

Disney PRESS
New York

Pleased to meet you, I am Bolt,
with a story just for you.
A tale of guts and inspiration—
every word of it is true.

Hey, over here! I'm Mittens.
I guess it is my fate
to tell you what REALLY happened
and to set the record straight.

I am a super-dog
possessing super power.

Why, my super bark alone
could stop a meteor shower!

Allow me to explain.
Bolt is a normal dog, you see.
He thinks he is a superhero,
but he just plays one on TV!

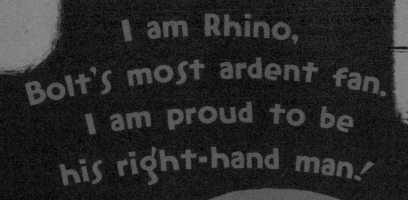

I am Rhino,
Bolt's most ardent fan.
I am proud to be
his right-hand man!

A superhero with a sidekick inside a plastic ball?

I can take you, evil cat, ALTHOUGH I MAY LOOK SMALL.

Behold my laser vision.

AND HIS PAWS OF STEEL.

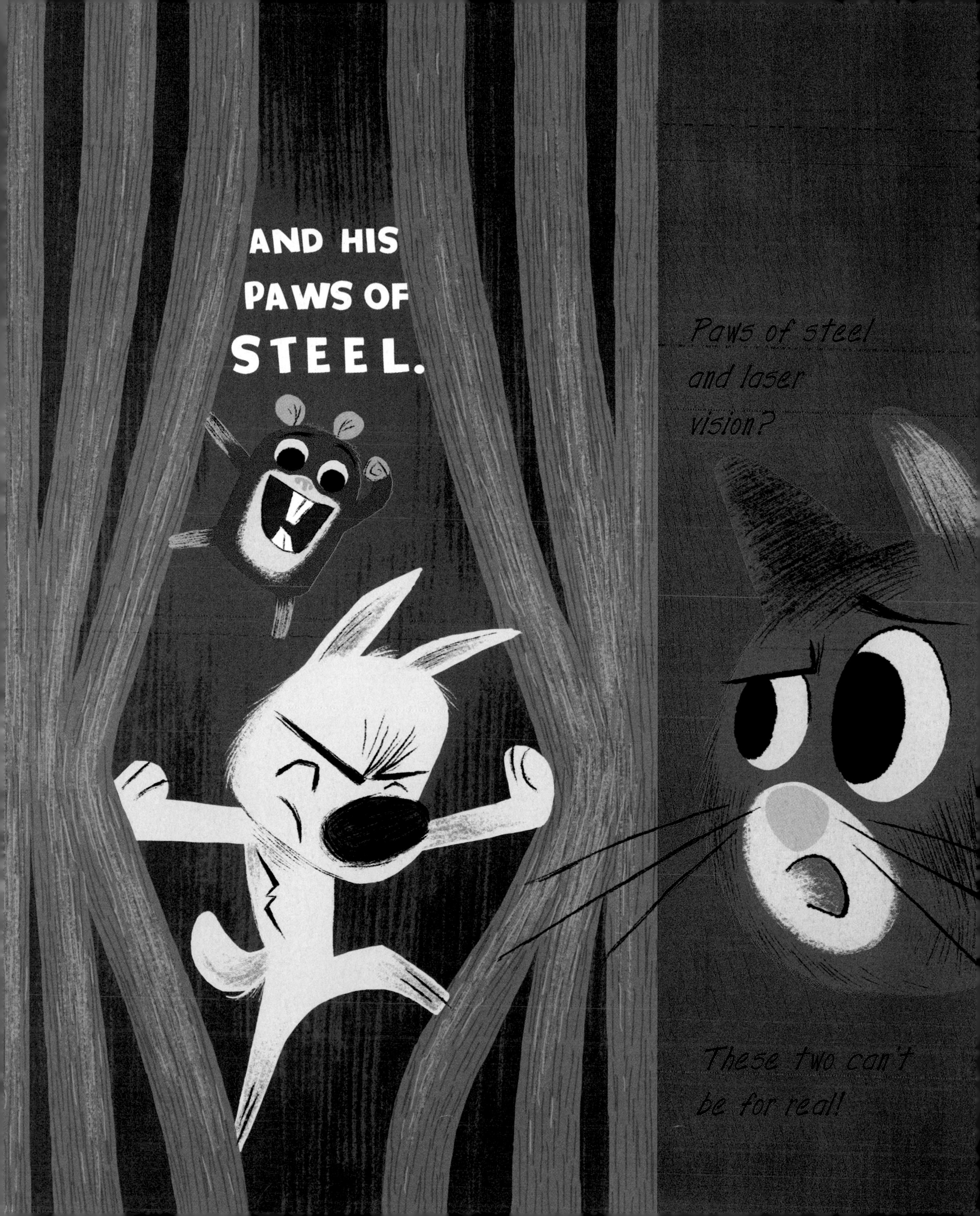

I can outrun speeding missiles, convince bad guys to do my bidding . . .

I cannot believe my ears.
You really must be kidding!

Running into cars head f i r s t,

SMASHING bridges left and right,

jumping over helicopters,

tossing speedboats out of sight.

The story is, I'm far from home,
and my person is in trouble.
I must get back to Hollywood
to save Penny ON THE DOUBLE.

WORLD ★ PORTLAND ★
ATLANTA ★ HOLLYWOOD ★ BUTTE ★ ALBUQUERQUE ★
PHOENIX ★ LAS VEGAS ★ DENVER ★
Bolt thinks I know where Penny is.
(Where did that come from?)
So now I am a prisoner.
That dog is SUPER dumb!
Vile vermin!
SECRET SPY!
Evil kitty!
Die! Die! Die!

So in my super way,
I devise a super plan.

Hmmm. . . .
Just how "super" is it
to sneak onto a moving van?

Then I move on to Phase 2:
To board a moving train.

I think this plan of yours
is totally insane!

No need to worry.
Bolt's crafty like a fox.
He's done this a jillion times
on the magic box.

We've almost made it home,
and now Mittens is in a bind.

But superheroes know
to leave no man
(or cat) behind!

Here I am, locked in kitty jail.
My chance at freedom? Zero.
Then Bolt shows up and sets
me free. . . .

ANIMAL
SHELTER

He IS a superhero!

Like where to put your head
while riding in a car.
(It's definitely a "dog thing."
I find it so bizarre.)

Or how to beg for dinner
with a sad look on your face.

How to bury tasty bones.

Or play fetch with a ball.

So THIS is what dogs do all day. I had no idea at all!

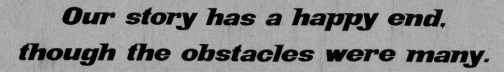

Our story has a happy end,
though the obstacles were many.

We made it home,
and I'm pleased to say
I found my person, Penny.

LOST DOG

LOST DOG

It never would have happened
if it weren't for these two,
I had my doubts, but I was wrong,
and they both pulled through.

Bolt may not have special powers,

but I'll admit he is quite super.

And Mittens is not vile vermin.

She is really quite a trooper!

Now that we are safe and sound,
we admit we made a fuss.

On this we all agree:

We were **ridonculous!**